Sir
Cumference

John Ryan

Young Piper Books
in association with Macmillan Children's Books

Clever Dick

Dick lived in a huge castle with his Uncle Cumference, who was the fiercest and bravest knight in the land.

His Aunt Lollipop's smart tea parties were almost as famous as her husband's valour.

But Dick was a big disappointment to both his aunt and his uncle.

He wasn't the least bit interested in fighting or entertaining. Instead of that . . .

. . . Dick was clever.
He read lots and lots of books.

He knew all the kings and queens of his country since the year dot.

Verigood the First
Verigood the Second
Verigood the Third
Queen Evenbetta
Veribad the First
Verigood the Fourth
Wurst the First
Wurst the Second...

He knew about geography and the
points of the compass,

which even his Uncle Cumference
sometimes found useful.

He could do sums,

which his Aunt Lollipop found useful too.

But mostly . . .

they didn't think much of him. They left him to do what he wanted at a safe distance at the other end of the castle.

MEANWHILE IN THE COUNTRY NEXT DOOR . . .

Sir Cumference's enemies were preparing to attack his castle.

The next night, as darkness fell, an
advance party sneaked up to
Cumference Castle.

They were carrying two huge tree
trunks, which they fixed in such a way
that the great gates were jammed
shut.

It was impossible to open them from the inside.

When Sir Cumference started to ride out for his morning charge

it ended in disaster.

That day the enemy army arrived and set up their camp in front of the castle. There was only one way in or out and that was through the gates.

Trapped on his battlements, Sir Cumference was red in the face with rage.

Normally he would have charged out and put the foe to flight all on his own,

but now all he could do was ride
round and round the castle yard,

getting angrier and angrier.

Sometimes he rode round the
battlements too, very nearly falling off
his horse.

But his enemies just stood around below the castle walls and laughed at him.

They felt quite safe, because they knew that Sir Cumference couldn't get out.

In the castle things got worse and worse. Sir Cumference stopped galloping about

and shut himself up in his study to play with his toy soldiers.

But all his games ended up with people stuck in castles surrounded by enemies.

Lady Lollipop got fed up with writing
invitations which she couldn't send
out, and laying tables
for guests who
would never come.

In fact the only happy person was
clever Dick, working away in his
chemistry vault.

In the end:

So Lady Lollipop made a huge white flag.

Sir Cumference was just taking it to hang out on the battlements, when Dick came running out of his workshop.

"Uncle Cumference! Aunt Lollipop!" he cried. "Come and look! I've got a surprise for you!"

It certainly was a surprise. Thirty gleaming glass balls lay neatly stacked on the floor.

"I've made catapults to throw them with," said Dick eagerly.
"Don't worry, we'll soon get rid of the enemy."

That night they set up the catapults in the castle yard. Outside the walls, confident of victory the next day, the enemy slept tight in their tents.

The effect was amazing. The foe were completely overcome by the terrible smells. Rubbing their eyes and holding their noses, they fled helterskelter through the night. By next morning . . .

PHE·E·W!

their camp was deserted.

Dick had been clever about the
weather, too. He knew that the
wind would be blowing the same
way as the enemy were fleeing,
so the smells went
with them.

The coast was clear at last.

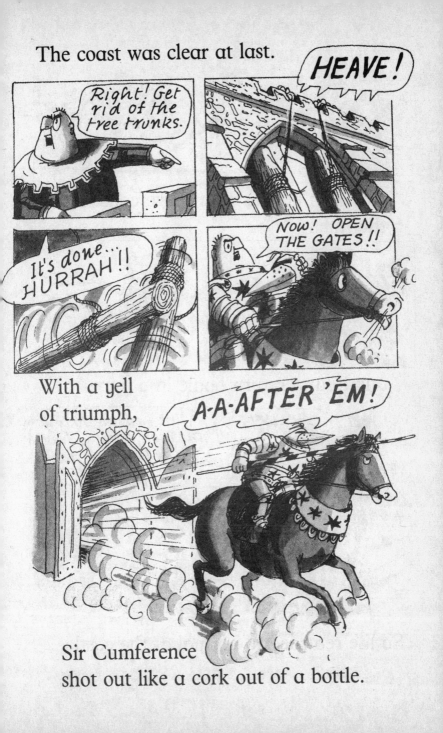

Sir Cumference
shot out like a cork out of a bottle.

But even he was nearly overcome by
the smell

and had to return home in a hurry.

So life returned to normal at the castle.

Sir Cumference was as warlike as ever,

and Lady Lollipop gave even more parties than before.

But now they were glad to have Dick carry on with his experiments, for nobody knew, after all . . .

when they might need his help again.

Titles in the FLIPPERS series

Now flip the book over
to read
SIR CUMFERENCE AND
LITTLE DAISY

Now flip the book over
to read
SIR CUMFERENCE AND
CLEVER DICK

First published 1990 by Macmillan Children's Books,
a division of Macmillan Publishers Ltd

This Young Piper edition published 1991 by
Pan Books Ltd, Cavaye Place, London SW10 9PG
in association with Macmillan Children's Books

9 8 7 6 5 4 3

© John Ryan 1990

The right of John Ryan to be identified as author of this
work has been asserted by him in accordance
with the Copyright, Designs and Patents Act 1988.

ISBN 0 330 31868 3

Printed and bound in Great Britain by
Cox & Wyman Ltd, Reading

The enemy were even more frightened
of Daisy

than they were of her uncle!

HURRAH!!

Of course, only Cumference knew what had *really* happened. Daisy promised never to tell a soul, but on one condition.

From then on, whenever Cumference rode out to war, he was not alone . . .

Promise?

Oh very well... BUT...

Naturally everybody thought it had been Cumference inside the armour. The King was so pleased that he gave his old friend an even grander title than before.

Arise BARON Cumference!

And mind you're not late for TEA again!

And one and all they fled back home again.

And that was how Little Daisy won the war without even striking a blow.

Of course when the enemy saw the armour, they thought it was Cumference approaching.

They were absolutely terrified!!

Then she set out from the castle, and rode straight at the enemy.

She was able to see by standing on the saddle and looking out through the visor.

Cumference wouldn't budge.

He went on playing with his toy soldiers.
It was then that Little Daisy saw her chance.

She ran to her uncle's great suit of starry armour,

climbed into it and had herself hoisted on to his charger.

Meanwhile, in the enemy capital:

Their chance had come at last. Gathering together their forces, they set off to attack the King.

It was the biggest and fiercest army he had ever faced.

He was very alarmed.

And of course the 'Lady' Lollipop was now just plain *Mrs* Cumference. That wasn't much fun either. She had to queue up in shops and wait her turn like everybody else. Nobody bothered to come to her tea parties any more.

Poor old Cumference. Life was now very different for him. Instead of doffing their caps and making way for him, people said things like

Hiya Cumfie!

Mornin' Mate!

and in the end he shut himself up in his study, and vowed that he would never fight for King and Country again. He would spend the rest of his life playing with his toy soldiers.

Then she told him what had happened.

The royal party arrived!

all day and all night. Then . . .

and that afternoon:

He had a really splendid day.

The few foemen who stayed to fight wished they hadn't.

The ones who ran away he chased . . .

"Make sure you're back in good time!
The King and Queen are coming to
tea."

And away he went. As usual, he was
wearing his shiny, starry armour.

One day the Lady Lollipop had a wonderful idea.

For a moment she felt quite alarmed.

A week later . . .

One thing she knew she must do. She ran to find Cumference, before he set out for his daily battle.

But Daisy couldn't knit, and hated sewing, and didn't want to cook.

This quite shocked her aunt's friends.

"A battlefield is no place for little girls," he used to say.

For once his wife agreed with him. "You shall stay at home with me, child," she said, "and learn nice lady-like pastimes . . ."

She was no good at all at helping with smart tea parties.

The only thing she *really* wanted to do was to ride out to war with her uncle.

But Cumference would have none of it.

YARR-RR-OO!!

Their niece Daisy was very wild and not at all lady-like. She spent her time whooping round the battlements and scaring the daylights out of her Aunt Lollipop.

But Sir Cumference had one weakness. He couldn't bear to let his enemies go. When they fled, he simply had to go after them. He chased them for miles and miles, and sometimes he didn't get back until the next day.

They knew exactly what he looked like, for his armour was always the same – huge and shiny, and inlaid with brightly coloured stars.

All his countrymen, from the King and Queen downwards, were very grateful to Sir Cumference. They knew that as long as he was around they were safe from enemy attack.

She invited all the best people, and she liked Cumference to be there to help hand things round.

But he could hardly do this if he was still out fighting or chasing the foe.

This made his wife,
the Lady Lollipop,
very cross.
She didn't think
much of her husband's
warlike zeal.

What she really enjoyed was having
huge tea parties.

Sir Cumference was the most fearless and ferocious fighter ever seen.

He was so terrifying that his enemies fled at the very sight of him.

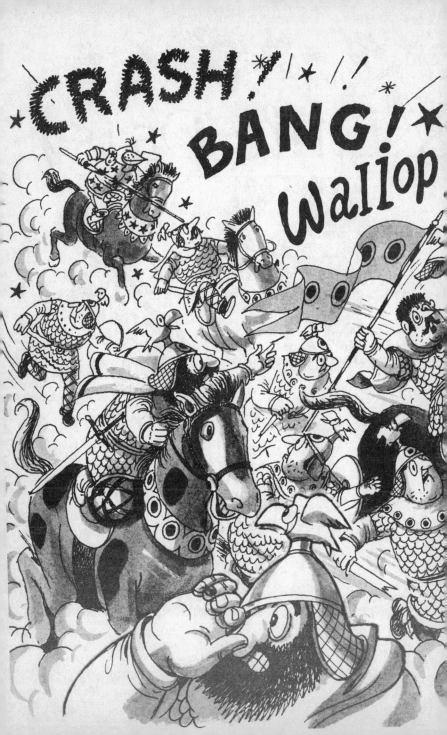

& Little Daisy

Sir
Cumference

John Ryan

Young Piper Books
in association with Macmillan Children's Books